MAGIC BOOMERANG

Throw it at a bad guy! It knocks him down and comes right back! *JUST LIKE MAGIC!*

No. 146

DINOSAUR

1/36TH SCALE!!

...s—not dug

No. 89

INVISIBLE-ISH INK

This ink will slightly hide your secret messages. Not completely though. Let's just all hope your enemies don't look too closely.

No. 28

MONSTER WIG

Be your most MONSTROUS self, but beware . . . it sheds! A lot! Comes in all colors of the rainbow except blue. (Blue is for Cookie Monster only.)

No. 112

ATOMIC ROARER

It's like a regular roarer— only more ATOMIC!

No. 139

SUPER SAFE SAFE

This safe will keep all of your stuff... well...safe. Hands down, the safest safe you can buy from us.

No. 492

FLIPPERS

No. 87

Good for scuba, snorkeling, or pretending to be a seal.

E-Z BREAK SAFE

This safe isn't nearly as good as the Super Safe Safe. Buy that one.

No. 262

SUPER CARD TRICK

This mesmerizing feat might hypnotize your victim—but probably not. Actually, definitely not.

No. 19

CHEMISTRY SET

This chemistry set might just give you super powers!*

No. 68

(*THIS CHEMISTRY SET DOES NOT GIVE YOU SUPER POWERS!!)

ANIMAL BELT BUCKLES

For all you heroes with animal powers, we've got buckles to match.

No. 88

CAT COMPASS

This cat compass can help you find true north or a feline companion.

No. 73

KNEE PADS

Keep your heroic knees scuff-free with this protective gear.

No. 22

No. 172

X-RAY GOGGLES

Look straight through walls or clothes. Perfect for finding a villain in hiding. Also great at parties.

No. 117

MEGA-WHISTLE

If you want to make noise, just pucker up and blow. The mega-whistle will do all the rest. Just remember to wear earplugs.

No. 76

CAPES, CAPES, MORE CAPES!

One cape, two capes, red capes, blue capes! Just the thing you need to look like a real superhero. Buy them by the dozen!

BEAR FEET

If you want to play bear but you're just not hairy enough, we've got the answer for you. Try these on and you can grin and bear it! Pardon the pun.

No. 37

KARATE-IN-A-BOX

Karate, Judo, Tae Bo, Krav Maga. All sorts of chops in just one box. Kicks not included.

No. 14

SUPER K OUTFITTERS

Rush me the items listed below to help me be a better hero (or villain— although that is not recommended; villains are evil). If I'm not 100% satisfied, I can return my purchase for a full refund.

NAME & ITEM NUMBER	HOW MANY	TOTAL

Name..

Address..

State.. Zip...................

Mr. PARTICULAR
THE WORLD'S CHOOSIEST CHAMPION

BY JASON KIRSCHNER

STERLING CHILDREN'S BOOKS
New York

Or when Kickin' Chicken attacked the Castle of Sandboxica . . .

FREEZE, FOUL FOWL!

KICKIN' CHICKEN

And he refused to spar with Dr. Slimyhands because he just didn't care for that shade of green.

EWWWWWW. NO WAY. I'M OUT!

LET'S GRAB THAT GOOPY GIR . . .

All that remained were the villainous Top 2! He knew he'd never survive a face-to-face encounter with anything green.

So he mustered his courage. He would try to beat . . . the squishy.

Just then, Mr. Particular noticed the Super-Duper Group assembled in the yard next door.

Mr. Particular was once again Defender of the Universe . . .

To my parents, who encouraged me,
to my wife, who believed in me,
and to my kids, who inspired me.

STERLING CHILDREN'S BOOKS
New York

An Imprint of Sterling Publishing
1166 Avenue of the Americas
New York, NY 10036

STERLING CHILDREN'S BOOKS and the distinctive
Sterling Children's Books logo are trademarks of Sterling Publishing Co., Inc.

The illustrations for this book were drawn with Prismacolor pencils
on paper and then digitally composed and colored.

ISBN 978-1-4549-1818-9

Distributed in Canada by Sterling Publishing
c/o Canadian Manda Group, 664 Annette Street
Toronto, Ontario, Canada M6S 2C8
Distributed in the United Kingdom by GMC Distribution Services
Castle Place, 166 High Street, Lewes, East Sussex, England BN7 1XU
Distributed in Australia by Capricorn Link (Australia) Pty. Ltd.
P.O. Box 704, Windsor, NSW 2756, Australia

For information about custom editions, special sales, and premium and corporate purchases,
please contact Sterling Special Sales at 800-805-5489 or specialsales@sterlingpublishing.com.

Designed by Merideth Harte and Richard Amari

Manufactured in China
Lot #:
2 4 6 8 10 9 7 5 3 1
02/16

www.sterlingpublishing.com

HAVE FUN WITH SOME OF THESE SUPER ITEMS!!!

AVIATION HELMET

Remember Amelia Earhart or Charles Lindbergh? No? Oh, well, they wore hats like this!

No. 4

MARTIAN HEADBAND

Wear this super-springy alien headband while you invade and conquer Earth for your spacey species! NOT FOR DOGS.

No. 96

TEENY-WEENY CAMERA

The best way to take teeny-weeny, itsy-bitsy spy photos.

No. 331

MYSTERY VILLAIN PACKAGE

Do you feel like being evil, but you're not sure how? This malevolent myste mixed bag comes with a spiteful super-villain identity, a corrupt costume, and a warped weapon. Cue evil laugh here!

No. 96

SUPER SUSPENDERS

When you see how well these things hold up your superpants, you'll have to suspend your disbelief!

No. 194

GLADIATOR HELMET

Conquer like a Roman or enter construction sites with no fear.

No. 57

DOUBLE DECODER WATCH*

Decrypt and decipher double the disastrous dilemmas. Also a compass!

(*Does not tell time.)

No. 61

RECODER WATCH*

Ruffle and rattle your enemies by recoding the codes you just decoded on your Double Decoder Watch. Wear one on each wrist.

(*Also does not tell time. Buy a clock.)

No. 62

BOX-O-SLIME

It's so easy to slime your enemies … and friends. Just add water for instant SLIME!

N

No.187

MAGNIFYING GLASS*

Great for clue hunting or for looking at the itsy-bitsy pics from the Teeny Weeny Camera. (*Not real glass.)

STOUTHEARTED SPYGLASS

Want to fight evil, but can't find any? Either give up—or extend your scope with this intrepid instrument.

No. 102

HERO DOCTOR KIT

Even heroes get hurt. Fix 'em up instantly! Bandages NOT included.

No. 207

NON-TRICK SOAP

No trick soap here! Heroes need to clean up after playing in the mud, and this soap will get you **sparkly** and **germ-free.**

HAWKIE WALKIE-TALKIES

These super-communicators help bird-themed heroes chat with their sidekicks and let bird-themed villains yell at their lackeys. Works up to a distance of 11 feet!

No. 216

FAUX YO-YO

This toy doesn't do anything a real yo-yo can, but from far away it looks real! Enjoy!

No. 008

No. 184

ZING RING*

Lots of heroes wear power rings! Then again, so do lots of moms. But their rings aren't power rings like the Zing Ring! ZING!

(*Ring does not power anything.)

No. 241

STEEL MARBLES

REAL STAINLESS STEEL!

Great for games or heroic inventions. Please—whatever you do—don't lose your marbles.

No. 222

FIVE-HERO TENT

Fit up to five heroes in this tent for a stupendous, super-ific sleepover. It's roomy and spacious and doubles as a super headquarters.

No. 215

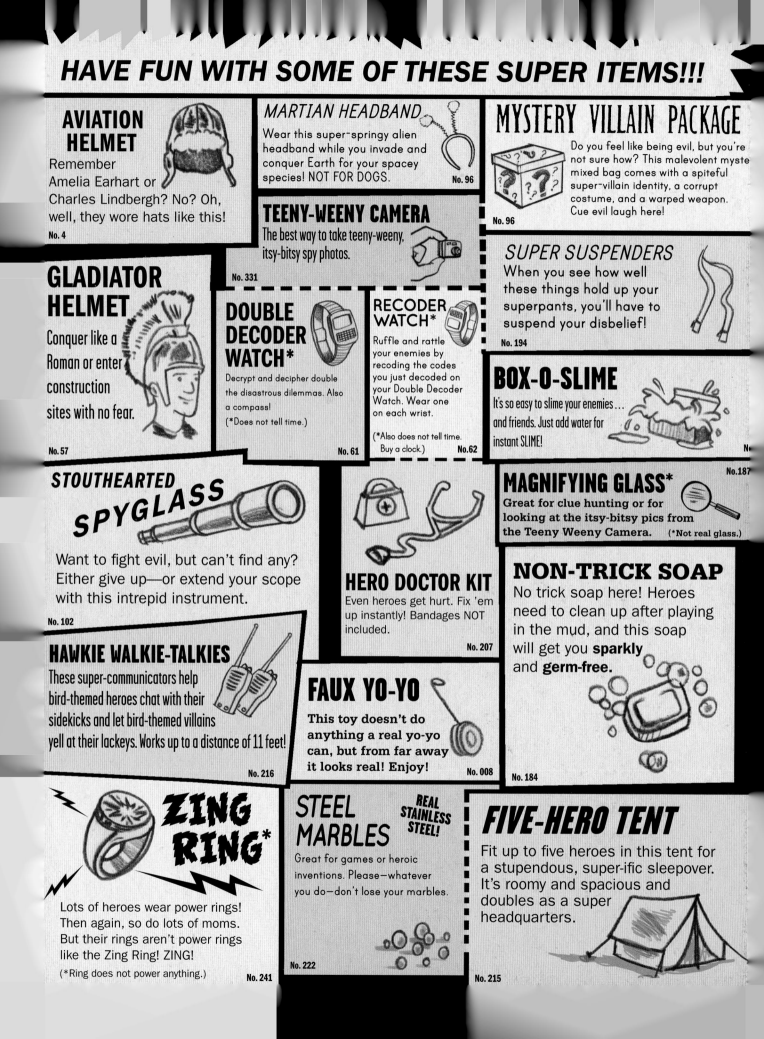